100

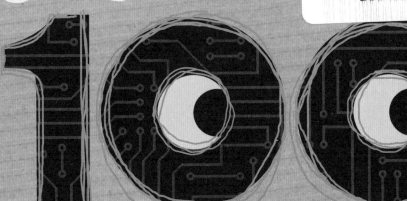

SECRET

missions

Be a legend. Accept them all.

Here arE your 100 missions, should you chOose to accept them.

TOP SECRET

There are only five rules:

1 When you complete a mission, record it in the book.

2 Never undertake a prank or spy mission on a stranger.

3 If you need something that does not belong to you for a mission, ask first.

4 Keep the missions secret. Lock this book when not in use.

5 Have fun. Be a legend.

Give yourself an alias

MISSION 1

Going undercover? You'll need one of these.

Your alias is your alternative name.

For a spy name, throw a die to pick a name from column A and column C. To convert it into an awesome wrestling name, throw a die to pick a name from column B to put in the middle.

Write your name below.

A	B	C
1. Blaze	1. The Rock	1. Jupiter
2. Hunter	2. The Hawk	2. Hilton
3. Max	3. The Storm	3. Hudson
4. Apollo	4. The Eagle	4. Spitfire
5. Conan	5. The Fox	5. Archer
6. Harley	6. The Shark	6. Typhoon

Now known as:

....

Surveillance

Tail a friend. Don't get caught.

Tell your friends you will be following one of them and recording their actions for 30 minutes sometime during the next week.

At your chosen time, grab a notebook and sneakily follow your chosen mark. Easy?

If he figures out he's being tailed, he should drop a tissue on the floor to indicate the game is up. At the end of the week, meet up to report back on your mission – successful sleuthing or failed following?

TOP TIPS

- Keep him in sight but don't follow him too closely, or you might get caught.
- Write down all the things he does in your notebook.
- Hide behind objects, corners or trees so he won't see you.

MISSION ACCEPTED | MONTH | DAY | YEAR |

Invent a secret cipher

Got classified information?

Ciphers are a great way to ensure secret messages are safe from enemy hands. You can create your own cipher by mixing up the alphabet or replacing letters with numbers or symbols.

Here is an example of a symbol alphabet:

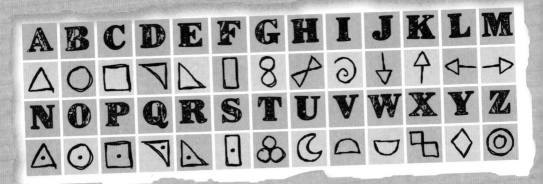

Write your own cipher here – use numbers, letters, symbols, or a mix of all three:

MISSION ACCEPTED

MONTH	DAY	YEAR

MISSION 4

WHAT'S next?

Can you crack the puzzle in under 60 seconds?

1 5 2 6 3 7 4 9 8

Answer at the back.

MISSION ACCEPTED MONTH | DAY | YEAR

Trail task

MISSION 5

Draw a pencil trail through the path without stopping or touching the sides in under 45 seconds.
If you touch the sides, you must erase the line and start again.

MISSION ACCEPTED MONTH | DAY | YEAR

tin can
challenge

Master a magnetic roll.

Ask an adult for a clean, empty ring-pull style tin can with no sharp edges. Make sure that a magnet sticks to the can first or this mission will not work.

1 Cut a strip of white paper the width of the can and long enough to wrap around it.

2 Draw cool designs and logos on the paper and stick it around the can.

3 Use string to mark out a track approximately 20 in (50 cm) long on a tabletop.

4 Hold the magnet in front of the can and use the magnetic force to roll the can along the track.

5 Your mission is to roll the can the length of the track without the can and magnet making contact.

MISSION ACCEPTED

MONTH	DAY	YEAR

Grow an extra finger

MISSION 7

Hold up your two index fingers at eye level and at arm's length. Relax your eyes and bring your hands slowly towards your face. Before long, your new, extra finger will appear floating in front of you!

Sick!

MISSION ACCEPTED | MONTH | DAY | YEAR |

Message drop

MISSION 8

Write a message in your secret code (see Mission 3) on a small piece of paper, fold it up and hide it in your living room. You must be able to reach the message without climbing on anything. Don't hide it near anything that is valuable or could be easily broken! Tell an accomplice where the message is hidden. He must pick up the message while the room is occupied and without anyone seeing what he is doing.

MISSION ACCEPTED | MONTH | DAY | YEAR |

9 DESIGN A
tattoo

Use your doodling skills to ink the arm.

LOVE

MONTH	DAY	YEAR

cone catch

Catch 'em if you can!

1 Roll a sheet of paper into a cone shape and tape it in place.

2 Scrunch up three pieces of paper into balls small enough to fit loosely into the upturned cone.

3 Using the cone as a launcher, your mission is to fire the balls into the air and catch all three back in the cone.

Epic win!

MISSION ACCEPTED | MONTH | DAY | YEAR

super **slurper**

Create a straw long enough to sip a drink from another room.

3 Take a handful of bendable straws. Pinch the end of one straw and gently push it into the top of another one to create a mega-straw long enough to reach another room.

1 Pour yourself a glass of water two-thirds full.

2 Pick a room (your bedroom or kitchen might be best) and place your drink near the door.

4 When you are ready, have a friend steady the straw in its glass, then go to the other end of the straw and enjoy your drink!

Mission accomplished!

MISSION ACCEPTED | MONTH | DAY | YEAR

Invent a secret language

MISSION 12

Disguise a message or make conversations impossible to understand by inserting two letters before the first vowel (A, E, I, O or U) in every word. An extra vowel and consonant (the word for all the other letters) works best – for example, "ad" or "it" or "ek" or "om."

Using "ad" this message . . .

I am going at three, meet me at the shops.

becomes:

Adi adam gadoing adat thradee, madeet made adat thade shadops.

Pick your two letters, then write and translate your messages below.

MISSION ACCEPTED

MONTH	DAY	YEAR

MISSION 13

CODEWORD X

You need an accomplice for this mealtime mission.

Your task is to use eight secret code words during the course of a meal.

The words must be used in communication between you and your mission partner. Whichever word you use, you must mean the opposite. So, if you say "delicious," you mean "gross," and if you say "gross," you mean "delicious."

Your mission is accomplished if you use all eight code words without raising your fellow diners' suspicions!

Sorted!

Boring	←---→	Exciting
Delicious	←---→	Gross
Hot	←---→	Cold
Fresh	←---→	Stale

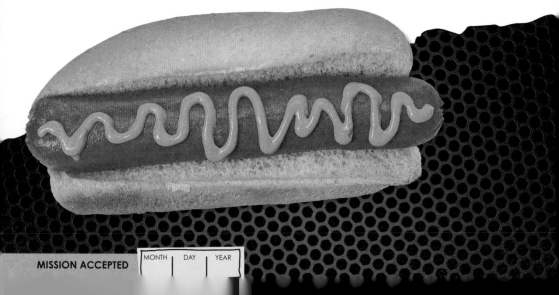

| MONTH | DAY | YEAR |

MISSION 14

Poker face

Can you make your opponent laugh?

Stand face-to-face with a friend. Without saying a word and by moving only your eyebrows and eyes, you must try to make each other laugh. See who cracks first. Best out of three is the champion.

MISSION ACCEPTED

MONTH	DAY	YEAR

ULTIMATE chocolate bar

MISSION 15

What would you put in it?

....
....
and
....
....
and
....

MISSION ACCEPTED

MONTH	DAY	YEAR

16

Shadow walking

Walk undetected in a friend's shadow.

1. This mission is the ultimate silent tailing test – practice with an accomplice first.

2. Stand as close as possible behind your accomplice so you're almost touching, then ask him to start walking.

3. Match your step to that of your accomplice so your feet are always just behind his.

4. When you're feeling confident, tell three friends that one of them will be shadowed at some point in the week.

5. If you manage to shadow your friend for 15 seconds without them noticing, your mission is accomplished!

TOP TIPS

- Lean backwards slightly so you cannot be heard breathing.
- If you match their walking pattern exactly, there is less chance of your footsteps being heard.

MISSION ACCEPTED

MONTH	DAY	YEAR

MISSION 17

INTERROGATION!

Can you uncover what your friend is thinking in ten questions?

Ask a friend to pick one of the subjects below, then think of an example. So if he picks TV shows, he might think of *The X Factor*.

You then can ask him up to ten questions to figure out what he is thinking. The snag is that you can only ask questions that can be answered by "yes" or "no."

For a tougher mission, reduce the number of questions to five.

subjects:

TV shows
Sports
Films
Music
Technology
Food
School
Games

MISSION ACCEPTED | MONTH | DAY | YEAR

MISSION 18 — Get on track

Design a cool training shoe!

Slick!

MISSION ACCEPTED

MONTH	DAY	YEAR

MISSION 19 — Total recall

Next time you and a friend watch your favorite show, ask him to think of five questions about the characters, the plot, or the setting of the show.

When the show is over, get him to ask the questions. Answer all the questions correctly and your mission is accomplished.

MISSION ACCEPTED

MONTH	DAY	YEAR

blindfold **guard**

Will you be caught snatching the snacks?

 Put some snacks in a shoe box.

 Attempt to take the box and get out of the room without making a sound.

 Blindfold a friend and get him to stand in the center of your room with the box at his feet.

 If he believes you are holding the box, he must pull off his blindfold. If you are caught touching the box, he has won. If he pulls off the mask when you are not touching the box or you get to the door without being challenged, your mission is accomplished and the snacks are yours!

MISSION ACCEPTED

MONTH	DAY	YEAR

sweet!

invisible ink

Leave an invisible message

The easiest way to write a secret message is to use a white wax candle as if it were a pen. Write your message between the lines of a "decoy message" such as a shopping list. Fold the message up and pass it to your accomplice.

He can only reveal the message by running over the page with a wipe-clean marker.

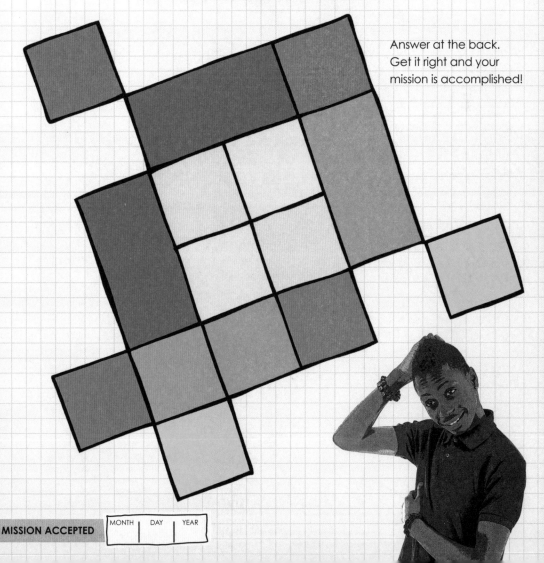

22 Where are the squares?

How many squares are there?

Answer at the back.
Get it right and your
mission is accomplished!

You must be joking!

23

Think of three endings to this classic joke.

I say, I say, I say, my dog's got no nose!

How does he smell?

❶ -------------------------------

❷ -------------------------------

MISSION ACCEPTED | MONTH | DAY | YEAR |

❸ -------------------------------

MISSION

24 TONGUE TWISTER

Read the rhyme in under ten seconds.

How much wood would a woodchuck chuck
if a woodchuck could chuck wood?
He would chuck, he would, as much as he could,
and chuck as much as a woodchuck would
if a woodchuck could chuck wood.

MISSION ACCEPTED | MONTH | DAY | YEAR |

Money grab

Is this mission impossible?

Beats me!

The aim is to snatch a dollar bill as it is dropped between your thumb and forefinger.

1 Rest your elbow on a table with your arm at a 45-degree angle to your body and your thumb and forefinger 1 in (3 cm) apart, like an open claw.

2 Get a friend to hold a dollar bill (use Monopoly money if you don't have one) so your fingers are either side of the note's midpoint.

3 Get your friend to drop the dollar without warning you first.

4 Try to catch the dollar between your fingers.

MISSION ACCEPTED

MONTH	DAY	YEAR

Walk through his mouth!

Stun your friends with this mouthwatering challenge.

MISSION **26**

1 Cut out the template on the reverse of the next page using the black dashed lines. Fold along the thick black line, and cut along each solid red line, stopping around 0.2 in (5 mm) from the fold.

2 Turn the paper over and cut along the dotted blue lines, starting at the fold and stopping 0.2 in (5 mm) from the opposite edge.

3 Unfold the paper, then cut along the thick black line, making sure you don't cut right to the edge at either end.

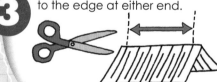

4 Carefully unfold the paper and place it over your head!

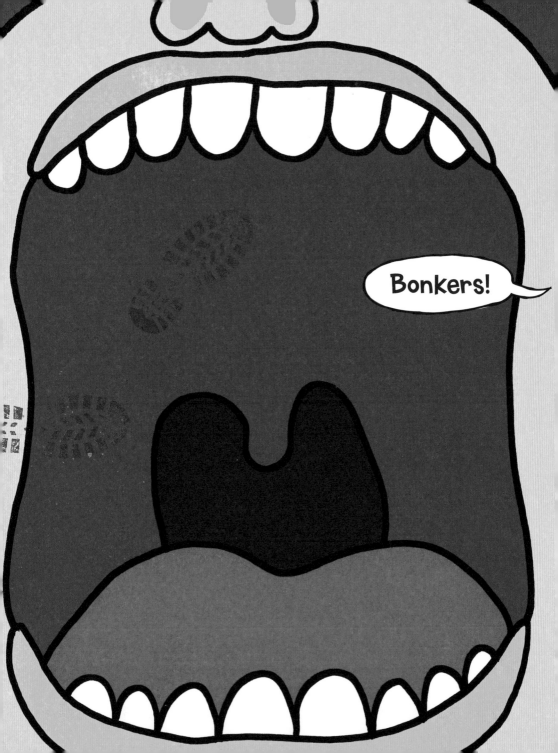

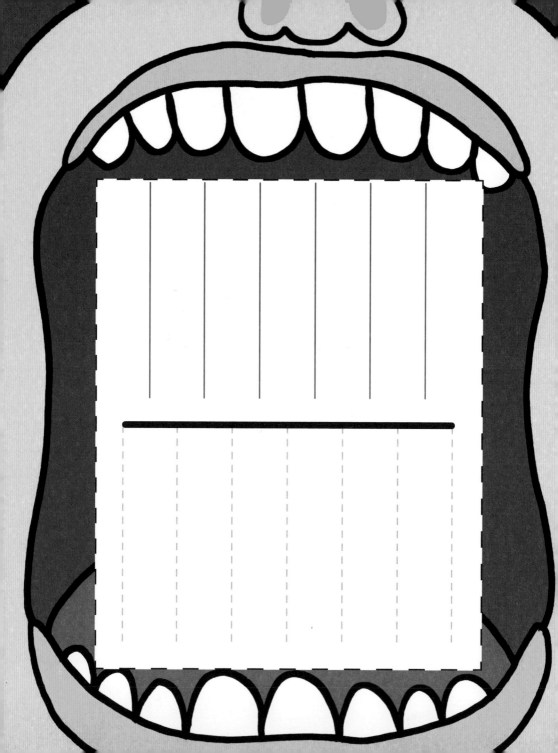

A-maz-ing

Master the maze in 30 seconds!

MISSION **27**

Begin at point A and use a pencil to draw a line to point B. Get from A to B in 30 seconds and your mission is accomplished.

A

B

MONTH	DAY	YEAR

28

IMPERSONATION

Can you fool a friend into thinking you are someone else?

1

Spend some time studying how a friend talks. Listen carefully to how he speaks and practice saying words in the same way. You should not exaggerate or make fun of his speech – just try to sound the same.

2

Make a note of any particular words and phrases he uses.

3

When you are ready, phone another friend, blocking your number so he cannot see who is calling.

4

Begin your impersonation. If you can fool your friend for 20 seconds, you have succeeded in your mission!

MISSION ACCEPTED

| MONTH | DAY | YEAR |

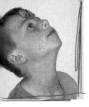

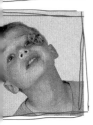
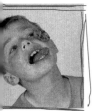
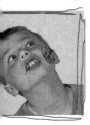

29

the **cookie** catch

Eat a cookie – the hard way!

Take a cookie of your choice and place it on your forehead. Get the cookie into your mouth without touching the cookie with your hands or allowing it to fall from your head.

TOP TIPS

- Tilting your head back will give the cookie greater stability on your head.
- Wiggling your eyebrows will help the cookie start its journey to your mouth.
- Don't go too fast or the cookie will be more likely to slip off.
- Try letting the cookie slip down one side of your face and use your cheek muscles to nudge it downwards.

Smooth!

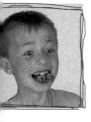

MISSION ACCEPTED | MONTH | DAY | YEAR |

Design
your own logo

30

Someday you might own your own company or sports brand. Design your own logo here. Try writing your initials and then adding designs around the letters.

MISSION ACCEPTED

MONTH	DAY	YEAR

MISSION 31

Count the **cords**

How many ropes can you see?

Answer at the back.

MISSION ACCEPTED	MONTH	DAY	YEAR

Don't say a word

MISSION 32

Pick a word from the list and get through a whole day without saying it once. Easy?

Choose one of these:

✗ **Yes**
✗ **No**
✗ **Your**
✗ **Why**
✗ **Sure**

MISSION ACCEPTED	MONTH	DAY	YEAR

Soapy boat race

MISSION

33

Who knew dishwashing liquid had amazing propelling powers?

1. Cut out the boats on the next page.

2. Find a large, shallow tray and pour in just enough water to cover the surface.

3. Pour some dishwashing liquid into an egg cup.

4. Place the first boat on the water, then use a toothpick to put a tiny blob of liquid into the boat's fuel tank. Watch it go!

5. Mark how far the boat sails by placing a coin along the side of the tray.

6. Pour the water away and wipe the tray dry, then repeat stages 2 to 5 to race the next boats.

Right on!

MISSION ACCEPTED | MONTH | DAY | YEAR

35 Observation test

Study this picture for one minute. Try to remember the details, such as how many birds there are in the sky and what the man is wearing. Now cover the picture and re-draw it in the empty box.

MISSION ACCEPTED | MONTH | DAY | YEAR |

MISSION

36 YEAR 3000
Picture yourself 1000 years from now.

I'm living in a ....

I'm on planet ....

My job is ....

I'm driving a ....

The most incredible thing about the year 3000 is

....

MISSION ACCEPTED | MONTH | DAY | YEAR |

37

the **paper** grab!

Pick up a newspaper from the floor with your teeth!

Stand a newspaper up on the floor. Stand on one leg, holding your left foot with your right hand. Without touching anything with your left hand, try to pick up the newspaper with your teeth!

MISSION ACCEPTED	MONTH	DAY	YEAR

38 WEB DESIGNER

Think of a name for your own website,
then draw its homepage here.

MISSION ACCEPTED

MONTH	DAY	YEAR

MISSION 39

Epic eruption!

Make a mini volcano, then watch it blow!

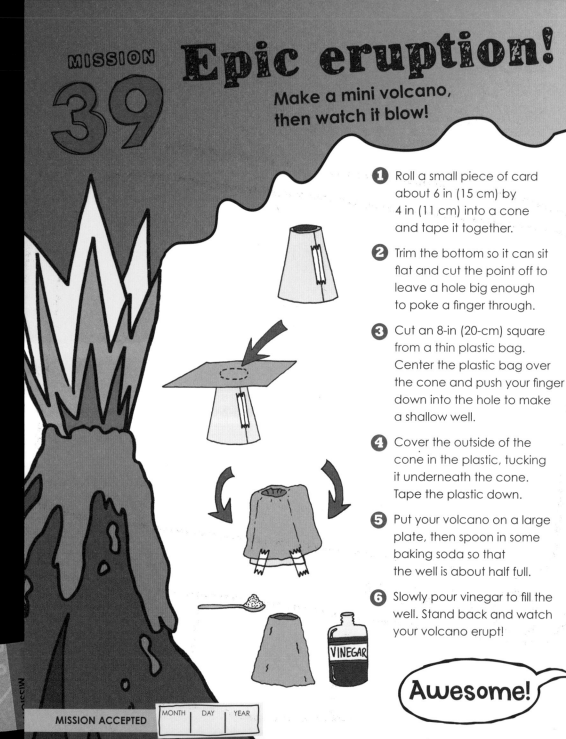

1. Roll a small piece of card about 6 in (15 cm) by 4 in (11 cm) into a cone and tape it together.

2. Trim the bottom so it can sit flat and cut the point off to leave a hole big enough to poke a finger through.

3. Cut an 8-in (20-cm) square from a thin plastic bag. Center the plastic bag over the cone and push your finger down into the hole to make a shallow well.

4. Cover the outside of the cone in the plastic, tucking it underneath the cone. Tape the plastic down.

5. Put your volcano on a large plate, then spoon in some baking soda so that the well is about half full.

6. Slowly pour vinegar to fill the well. Stand back and watch your volcano erupt!

Awesome!

VINEGAR

MISSION ACCEPTED | MONTH | DAY | YEAR

MISSION 40 Make your own tomato spiders

Tomato stalks look strangely like spiders!

Get a nice supply by saving the stalks whenever you have a salad. When you have a good collection, color them with a black marker and leave them around the house as a spooky surprise for your family.

MISSION ACCEPTED

MONTH	DAY	YEAR

MISSION 41 CRACK THE COLOR CODE!

Which color comes next: yellow, blue, or black?

Brown　　Green　　Orange　　Purple　　Red　　..............

MISSION ACCEPTED

MONTH	DAY	YEAR

Answer at the back.

42
magic
wheels

Can you make them move?

Hold the page so that the wheels are at eye level. Look at one wheel and move the page slowly towards your eyes. The other wheels should turn!

MISSION ACCEPTED

MONTH	DAY	YEAR

WHAT COMES NEXT?

MISSION
43

Figure out which letters come next.

Answer at the back.

AZCXEVGT _ _

MISSION ACCEPTED

MONTH	DAY	YEAR

Rule the school!

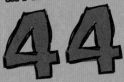
44

If you could introduce any new class subject for your school, what would it be? Write it on the board!

MISSION ACCEPTED | MONTH | DAY | YEAR |

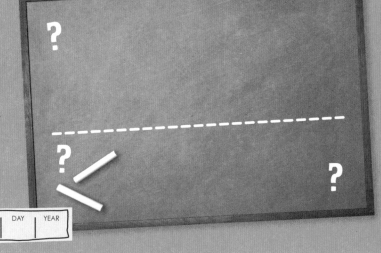

MISSION
45

Pen puzzle

Make ten out of nine pens.

Grab nine pens and make ten out of them. You might have to think out of the box for this one!

MISSION ACCEPTED | MONTH | DAY | YEAR |

Answer at the back.

MISSION 46

Ultimate pet!

Invent your ultimate pet. Pick three animals from the list, then name your pet by mashing up the words. For example, a **doferrat** is part dog, part ferret, and part rat.

- ☐ Dog
- ☐ Ferret
- ☐ Rat
- ☐ Gerbil
- ☐ Cat
- ☐ Hamster
- ☐ Terrapin
- ☐ Iguana

My ultimate pet is called:

....

MISSION ACCEPTED | MONTH | DAY | YEAR |

MISSION 47

Morning muddle

Cause cereal confusion with this early-morning prank!

1 Take a cereal box and remove the bag containing the cereal.

2 Carefully peel away the glued-down edge of the box so that you end up with a flat piece of cardboard.

3 Put the box back together inside out and use double-sided sticky tape to secure the edges you separated earlier. Leave the top flap unstuck so that it can still be opened!

4 Put the cereal bag back in the box, and fold the top flap down to close it.

5 Put the box back in the cupboard and wait for the reaction.

MISSION ACCEPTED | MONTH | DAY | YEAR |

48 sandwich max

Doodle the fillings.

Tasty!

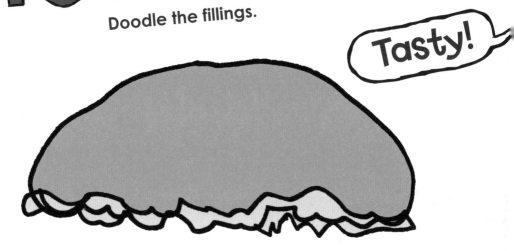

Secret WORDSEARCH

There is a ten-word message hidden in the wordsearch.
Your mission? Find it! Words can be found across and down.

T	H	E	G	M	A	N	S	I	O	N	H
N	F	S	T	I	G	A	U	D	X	R	Y
G	A	B	H	F	E	U	J	K	A	T	C
U	Q	I	K	N	M	L	S	O	H	J	
N	R	G	T	Y	E	N	T	E	R		
S	T	K	S	P	A	U	Z	J	N		
Y	T	V	F	V	D	N	T	B			
		C	J	W	I	L	L				
		H	N	Y	T						
		E	H	Z							
		F	U	A							

As you find the words
write them on the pad,
then rearrange them
into a sentence.

The secret message is:

....

....

Answer at the back.

MISSION ACCEPTED

| MONTH | DAY | YEAR |

MISSION 50

Suction POWER

Pass on a dollar without using your hands!

1 Take a dollar bill (use Monopoly money if you don't have one) and lay it on a table between you and a friend.

2 Take a straw each.

3 Suck through the straw to lift the dollar off the table.

4 Your friend must then use the straw and his own suction power to take the dollar from you without it falling to the table.

TOP TIP

The mission will not work if you are both sucking on your straws at the same time!

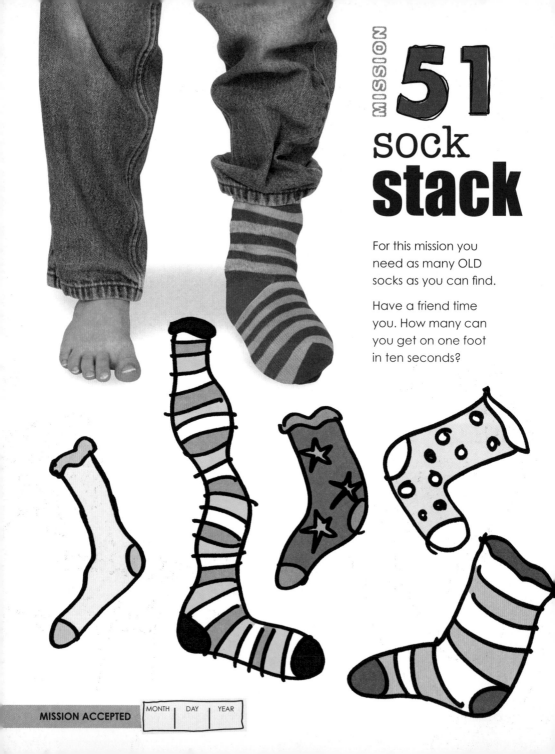

MISSION 51
sock
stack

For this mission you need as many OLD socks as you can find.

Have a friend time you. How many can you get on one foot in ten seconds?

MISSION ACCEPTED | MONTH | DAY | YEAR |

family 52
detective

Find the answers to the
questions without anyone
suspecting you are
undertaking a secret survey.

Who is the youngest member of your family?

Who is the oldest member of your family?

Has anyone in your family ever lived abroad?

Who is the most famous member of your family?

Who is the tallest member of your family?

Who is the best singer?

Who is the worst dancer?

Who is the best comedian?

Who is the worst cook?

MISSION ACCEPTED

| MONTH | DAY | YEAR |

53 Fierce FLIGHT!

Make your own stunt plane!

Follow the instructions to make your glider, then challenge a friend to make their own competing craft. Hold races, stunt shows, and distance trials. Thick paper is good for stunts, thin paper for long, graceful glides.

1

Fold the paper in half to make a center crease, and unfold.

2

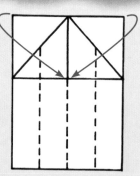

Fold the top corners down to meet at the crease.

3

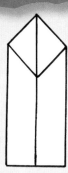

Fold the two sides in to meet at the crease using the lines shown in step 2.

4

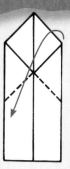

Fold the top right edge over to form the crease shown, and unfold.

5

Do the same on the opposite side, and unfold.

6

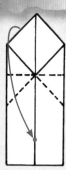

Fold the top down to the point marked to form a horizontal crease, and unfold again.

7

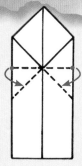

Bring the points shown together and, letting the top come down to form a diamond shape, fold down flat.

8

Fold the point shown up to form the crease shown.

9

Fold this triangle back the other way and tuck under the folds made in step 7 to form a sturdy pocket.

10

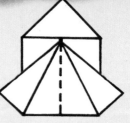

Fold the two flaps at the bottom outwards.

Your glider is ready to fly!

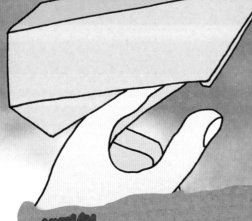

TOP TIPS

- Hold the pocket with your fingers inside and your thumb underneath and throw it gently for optimum gliding capacity.
- Try holding either side of the plane with your thumb and fingers and throwing it faster for spectacular stunts.
- Experiment with extra twists and folds to alter the glider's performance.

MISSION ACCEPTED

MONTH	DAY	YEAR

MISSION 54
MOVIE MAGIC!

Write the name of your favorite movie on the board. Now think of a name for the sequel.

FAVORITE FILM:

_____

SEQUEL:

MISSION ACCEPTED | MONTH | DAY | YEAR

MISSION 55
super **speed** talking

Your mission: pass this message on in under five seconds.

"Meet the agent in the park on the green bench next to the tree at seven o'clock. Do not forget to give him the case and do not say a word."

MISSION ACCEPTED | MONTH | DAY | YEAR

56 LIVE DROP

Pass a message to your accomplice without him or anyone noticing!

1 Write your note and fold it up.

2 Tell your accomplices that at some point during the day you will drop a secret message into one of their pockets.

3 Pick a time when your chosen accomplice is with a group of other friends.

4 Walk past the group, casually dropping the note into his pocket. Then walk away.

5 If nobody, including your accomplice, notices you drop the message, your mission is accomplished.

TOP TIPS

- Walk slowly but purposefully past your accomplice – this will give you time for the drop.
- Ignoring your accomplice would raise suspicions, but you must not stop walking so a nod and a "hi" is enough.
- Look ahead at all times – looking down at your hands or at your friend's pocket will raise suspicions.

MISSION ACCEPTED

MONTH	DAY	YEAR

Pencil darts!

Study the dartboards, then read all the instructions before you try this mission.

1. Take a pencil and close your eyes tightly.

2. Hold the pencil point down above the page, twirl it three times, then press the pencil down so it makes a mark on the page. Be sure to keep your eyes closed.

3. Do this six times, ensuring you try out every board, then open your eyes and count up your scores. Your mission is to score over 100.

MISSION ACCEPTED

MONTH	DAY	YEAR

MISSION

58

mirror writing

Find a mirror to read the message.

Once you have worked out this message, write your name in mirror writing. To give you a hand, here's the alphabet:

Write here

a b c d e f g

h i j k l m

n o p q r s t

u v w x y z

Noel

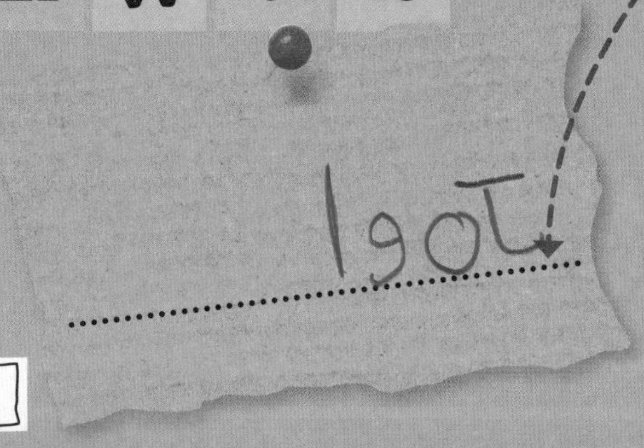

MISSION ACCEPTED | MONTH | DAY | YEAR |

Join the dots

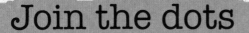

MISSION
59

Connect the dots
using just four
straight lines and
without taking your
pencil off the paper.

● ● ●

● ● ●

● ● ●

MISSION ACCEPTED MONTH | DAY | YEAR

Answer at the back.

MISSION
60 DESERT-ISLAND dilemma

You are being
sent to a desert
island. It has solar
electricity, fresh
water, and food
supplies. You can
take just three
things with you.
What will they be?

1 ....

2 ....

3 ....

MISSION ACCEPTED MONTH | DAY | YEAR

GROUNDED?

Make a secret emergency supply kit, just in case.

Find an old shoe box. Gather together a magazine you haven't read, snacks, cookies, and soda or juice in cartons. Put all the items in the box, along with any other items you think you might need in a grounded emergency.

Seal the box with a strip of paper or tie it up with string, so if any prying eyes take a peek inside, you'll know about it! Hide the box under your bed. Retrieve the box and break the seal in emergencies only!

MISSION ACCEPTED | MONTH | DAY | YEAR

---

62 OUT OF THIS WORLD

Imagine that you've discovered a new planet. Now you need to name it. Think of a name using the following three letters in the order below (but not together), adding as many extra letters as you want.

G O B

MISSION ACCEPTED | MONTH | DAY | YEAR

Parent trap!

See if someone's been snooping at your stuff!

1 Protect your drawers. Pull a hair from your head, trimming it so it's about 1.5 in (4 cm) long. Cut a small piece of tape and stick the hair to the inside of a drawer. Gently fold the hair down and close the drawer. You'll know if the drawer has been opened because the hair will have popped out and will be visible from the outside of the drawer.

2 Put a small piece of folded paper inside the door hinge when you leave your room and close the door. If anyone enters while you're gone, the paper will fall to the floor.

3 Trail a length of thick cotton thread on the floor around your bed. If anyone snoops under your bed, they will move the cotton.

4 Leave a pile of dirty laundry in front of your closet door. Place two smelly socks on the top in a cross. If anyone snoops in your closet, they'll disturb the pile and never be able to put it back as you left it!

MISSION ACCEPTED | MONTH | DAY | YEAR |

MISSION 64 — EXTRAORDINARY ANIMALS

Find out which are real and which are fake.

	REAL	FAKE
Giant coconut crab	☐	☐
Moss piglet	☐	☐
Dog-eared weevil	☐	☐
Glass frog	☐	☐
Flat-tailed mountain duck	☐	☐

MISSION ACCEPTED | MONTH | DAY | YEAR

Answers at the back.

Auto design — MISSION 65

Using the wheels as a starting point, design and name your dream car.

MISSION ACCEPTED | MONTH | DAY | YEAR

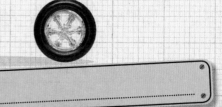

66 Bedroom golf

Score a hole in one!

Place the book flat on the floor with this page face up.

Make a golf club by tightly rolling up a piece of 8 ½ in (21.5 cm) by 11 in (28 cm) paper and folding the end over to make its head. Scrunch up a piece of paper for your ball and you are ready to play.

Decide on a teeing-off point at least 20 in (50 cm) away and aim for the hole. Land on the hole in as few shots as possible. If you land in the bunker, the rough, or the water hazard, you must start again.

rough

water hazard

bunker

Fore!

MISSION ACCEPTED

MONTH	DAY	YEAR

67 Hidden MESSAGE

Hide a secret message in a seemingly random page of letters.

1. Cut out a 6-in (15-cm) square of paper.

2. Your message should be short and simple – for example, "Meet by the library."

3. Count the letters and make that number of hole punches in the paper. The holes should be spaced apart roughly in rows.

4. Place the punched paper directly over another sheet of paper the same size so that the corners line up.

5. Write your message in the holes, then remove the punched paper and fill in the gaps with random letters.

6. The only way a friend can decipher your message will be by lining up the punched-paper decoder over the scrambled letters.

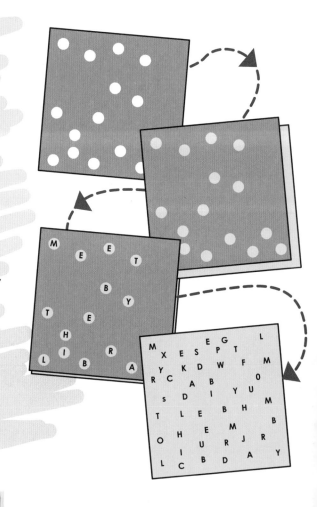

68

Cookie

challenge!

For this mission you need 19 mini cookies (ask permission before you take them) and a die. Your mission is to build a tower in four throws of the die.

1 Put one cookie on a table in front of you and throw the die three times.

2 After each throw, add the number of cookies shown on the die to the tower.

3 If after three throws the tower has not toppled, you have completed your mission.

MISSION ACCEPTED

MONTH	DAY	YEAR

MISSION 69

Alien **invasion!**

Stage an outer-space earth attack.

Find a camera, then go to the back of the book and cut out the alien. Create a slot at the bottom of its body – the easiest way is to pinch the base together and cut along the dotted line.

Put the tip of your finger through the slot and hold the alien in front of you at eye level. Position the camera so the alien appears to be part of the scene.

Your mission is to picture the alien in the following locations. This is a covert mission: your victims must not know that they are under attack!

Visiting the bathroom

Falling on a parent's head

Landing in your dinner

Sneaking under a friend's bed

MISSION ACCEPTED   MONTH   DAY   YEAR

Mind reader

Convince your friends you can read their thoughts!

MISSION

70

For this mission you will need an accomplice and an audience.

1 Choose nine objects (square or rectangular objects like playing cards are best) and arrange them in a grid.

2 Go out of the room while a member of your audience chooses an object. He must tell the group what it is very quietly so that you cannot hear.

3 When called, come back in. Your accomplice then points to each item at random asking, "Is it this one?"

4 As soon as your accomplice points at the chosen object, you tell your audience that it is the right one.

How do you do it?

Easy! Your accomplice secretly shows you where the chosen object is located on the grid. He does this by pointing to the appropriate point on the first object. For instance, if the chosen object is in the bottom right-hand corner of the grid, your accomplice first points to the bottom right-hand corner of the first object.

No one else will notice, but you now know where the object is, so when your friend points to it, you can amaze everyone with your mind-reading skills!

MISSION ACCEPTED   MONTH | DAY | YEAR

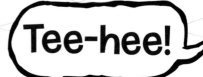
Tee-hee!

Sickly **surprise!**

The easiest way to make a beastly barf!

1 Ask to take a pack of cup soup – you'll need one or two teaspoons.

2 Squirt a blob of PVA glue onto a square of plastic wrap or flattened plastic bag.

3 Sprinkle the soup over the glue and mix it in with an old plastic spoon.

4 Let the glue set overnight. When it's ready, it should peel off easily and feel like plastic.

MISSION ACCEPTED

MONTH	DAY	YEAR

72 Zip it!

Find a friend and hold a conversation for two minutes without opening your mouth.

MISSION ACCEPTED

MONTH	DAY	YEAR

73 Eagle eyes

Study the pictures and find three differences.

MISSION ACCEPTED

MONTH	DAY	YEAR

Answers at the back.

MISSION 74 SECRET MINI MESSAGE

Meeti...
my hou...
o'clock with
the files.

Tyler Scott
237 Park Street

1 Take an envelope and a self-adhesive stamp.

2 Lightly draw a square just smaller than the stamp in the top right corner. Write your secret message in the square then cover it neatly with clear tape.

3 Write "thought you might find this interesting" on a sticky note and stick it to a page torn from a magazine. Put the page in the envelope and seal it. Stick the stamp over the tape, covering your message.

4 Address the envelope to your friend and mail the message.

5 When your friend receives the message, he can open it in full view without raising suspicions, then when no one is around, he can peel off the stamp to reveal the secret message.

MONTH	DAY	YEAR

Secret spy paper

Make this easy piece of essential spy kit.

Find an old newspaper, open it up and, using a pencil, make a hole halfway up the page and about 4 in (10 cm) from the side. Hold the paper with your finger over the hole. When you need to snoop secretly, hold the page up and move your finger away from the hole.

MISSION ACCEPTED

MONTH	DAY	YEAR

Mystery Agent

MISSION 76

Find the name of the secret agent hidden in this message. All the letters spelling his name are in the correct order and in the same place in each word.

Are **DoGS AnD miCE** b**lue, red Or White n**o**w?**

Agent's name:

....

MISSION ACCEPTED

MONTH	DAY	YEAR

Answer at the back.

Frogolympics

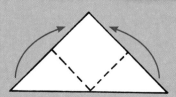

Follow the instructions to make
two jumping frogs, then find a
friend and let the games begin!

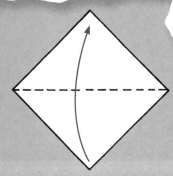

Fold a square piece of paper
in half along the diagonal.

Fold the two corners up
to the top.

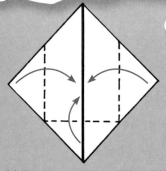

Fold the two corners at the sides
to meet in the middle, and the
bottom to meet at the same
point, to look like an envelope.

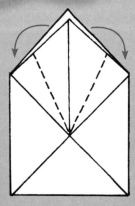

Fold the top two flaps
outwards so the edges meet
the flaps on the left and right.

5

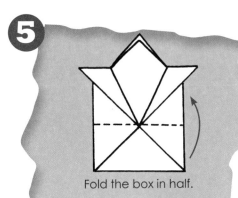

Fold the box in half.

6

Fold in half again, downwards. Don't forget to give your frog some eyes!

Press on the rear edge of the frog's back to make it jump. Experiment with finger control to make the frog jump higher or further, and test different sizes of paper for optimum performance!

Construct Frogolympic events. For instance:

• Create a high jump with three straws joined in an H-shape with sticky tack. How high can you raise the bar?

• Cut straws down to create a hurdles track. Who has the fastest finger?

• Place a plastic bowl in front of the frogs and compete to be the first to flick your frog into the "pool."

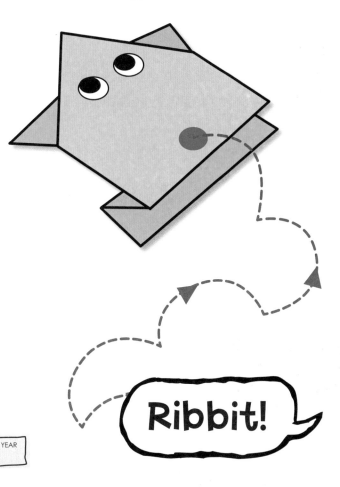

Ribbit!

MISSION ACCEPTED | MONTH | DAY | YEAR

Milk**shake**

Invent three milkshake flavors.

Slurp!

Strawberry 'n' ....

Chocolate 'n' ....

Cookie 'n' ....

MISSION ACCEPTED | MONTH | DAY | YEAR

MISSION 79 Solve the mystery

? ? ? ?

There are two stones and a carrot in an empty field. Nobody has been to the field since winter. How did they get there?

MISSION ACCEPTED | MONTH | DAY | YEAR

Answer at the back.

Study the scene

Three things are wrong – find them.

Answers at the back.

1 _____

2 _____

3 _____

MISSION ACCEPTED	MONTH	DAY	YEAR

MISSION 81 — SLY SPY

Peripheral vision – that's everything you can see out of the corners of your eyes – is an essential skill for covert snooping.

1. Looking directly ahead, get your friend to stand to one side of you so you can only see him out of the corner of your eye, and ask him to hold up some fingers or make a face at you.

2. Call out how many fingers he is holding up, or what face he is making, without moving your eyes or head. Practice to make your peripheral vision perfect!

MISSION ACCEPTED | MONTH | DAY | YEAR |

Utter ~~horsense~~ *non*sense!

MISSION 82

Put words into the horse's mouth.

MISSION ACCEPTED | MONTH | DAY | YEAR |

83 Cool kit!

Design a new uniform for your team.

Cool!

MONTH	DAY	YEAR

84 Barber BRAINTEASER

There were only two barbers in the town of Bubworth: Pete and Bob. Pete's hair was always a mess, while Bob's cut was super neat. Which barber would you go to?

Answer at the back.

MISSION ACCEPTED | MONTH | DAY | YEAR

Pete

Bob

Calculated message

MISSION

85

Numbers become letters when tapped into a calculator and turned upside down. Translate the numbers in the calculator into letters, then rearrange them to find the name of something you need for outdoor missions.

Answer at the back.

MISSION ACCEPTED | MONTH | DAY | YEAR

MISSION 86 Chip challenge

Find chips or snacks in four different flavors. Put a few of each into four separate bowls. Put on a blindfold and ask a friend to switch the bowls around. Taste the chips – your challenge is to name each snack correctly without peeking.

MISSION ACCEPTED

MONTH	DAY	YEAR

Secret password

MISSION 87

Keep your space private – invent a secret password. Share it with your allies and make a sign for your door: **Private! Knock twice then entry by password only!**

1 Write down your first and last names.

2 Make as many words as you can from the letters. For example, from Ryan Scott's name you can make:

rot	can	nay	stay
ants	tan	toys	ran

3 Pick one of the words as your password or use the words to make a stupid sentence. So Ryan's secret password could be "Ants can tan."

KEEP OUT

My password is:

....

MISSION ACCEPTED

MONTH	DAY	YEAR

88

Secret **sneak** peeks

Peek around corners without being detected!

1 Ask permission to use a small mirror – one from an old makeup kit is ideal.

2 Find a nice, sturdy stick – about 12 in (30 cm) long and 0.8 in (2 cm) thick. This will be your handle. If you cannot find a stick, use a ruler.

3 Using strong tape (gaffer tape is best), attach one end of your stick to the back of the mirror.

4 Practice round-the-corner snooping with a friend. Ask him to stand in the middle of a room in different positions, while you lurk by the doorway, making a note of his actions.

MISSION ACCEPTED | MONTH | DAY | YEAR |

Going undercover

Become a master of disguise!

When undertaking secret missions, a disguise is sometimes essential.

Follow these tips to fool your friends:

1 Brush your hair in a different way.

2 Wear dark glasses.

3 Change the way you stand: slouch, put your weight on one leg, or straighten your back.

4 Wear a wig.

5 Try a fake beard or moustache.

6 Try different hats.

7 Put scrunched-up paper in your shoes – this will encourage you to walk differently.

8 Always carry a large handkerchief. If you think someone might recognize you, hold the handkerchief to your face and pretend to be blowing your nose.

9 Carry a bag with spare glasses, hats, scarves, and a hairbrush so you can change your disguise at a moment's notice!

For the ultimate disguise, invent a whole new character for yourself with a new name, age, and way of speaking.

My undercover name will be:

....

MISSION ACCEPTED | MONTH | DAY | YEAR |

Secret spiral

MISSION 90

The ultimate low-tech message scrambler!

1. First cut a strip of paper about 12 in (30 cm) by 0.5 in (1 cm).

2. Carefully wrap the paper around a pencil.

3. Write your message along the pencil, being careful to write within the edges of the paper.

4. Unravel the paper and fill in the blank space with random letters.

5. Roll the paper up tightly and pass it to your accomplice.

   The message can only be read if it is rolled around a pencil that is the same size.

MISSION ACCEPTED | MONTH | DAY | YEAR |

91 ALIEN ATTACK

Fill in the speech bubbles to create an epic adventure.

MISSION ACCEPTED

MONTH	DAY	YEAR

Neat!

Bizarre banana

Fool a friend with a sealed, pre-sliced banana!

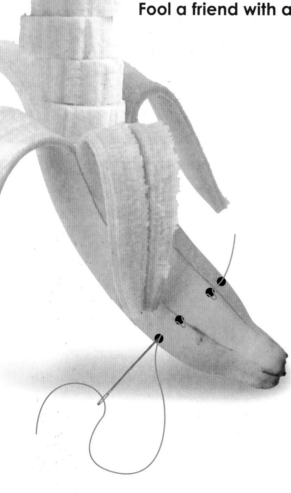

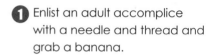

1. Enlist an adult accomplice with a needle and thread and grab a banana.

2. Carefully push the threaded needle through one of the ridges in the banana, making it come out of the next ridge along.

3. Make sure to leave some thread hanging out of the first hole.

4. Pushing the needle back into the same hole, repeat step 2. Do this until you have threaded the whole banana and the needle has come back out of the first hole.

5. Grab the two ends of thread hanging out of the same hole and pull them both slowly until the thread comes all the way out.

6. Do this for as many slices as you want.

7. Return the banana to the fruit bowl or offer it to a friend.

8. Watch their surprise when the banana is revealed ready-sliced!

MISSION ACCEPTED

MONTH	DAY	YEAR

Your mission is to design the best bedroom gadget ever.
Automatic bed-maker? Cinema-screen wall?
Never-ending popcorn machine? Electric curtains?
Invent it here!

Name of brilliant invention:

Best features and what it can do:

MISSION ACCEPTED | MONTH | DAY | YEAR |

94 Bean **bonanza!**

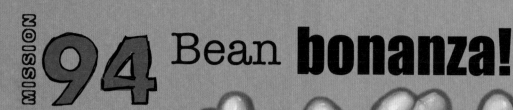

There's a whole lot of beans on this page. Your mission: count them all in under ten seconds.

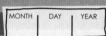

Answer at the back.

MISSION ACCEPTED | MONTH | DAY | YEAR

Balance a broom

Make a broom stand up on its own!

Find a flat-bottomed broom and stand it up on its bristles. It may help to press down on the handle gently so the bristles spread out either side. Shift the broom until you can find where it will balance then slowly and gently remove your hands.

95

Awesome!

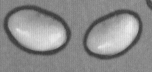

MISSION ACCEPTED | MONTH | DAY | YEAR

Disguise the spies

Draw hats, moustaches, glasses, beards, spots, and scars to prepare the spies for undercover action.

MISSION ACCEPTED

MONTH	DAY	YEAR

Calculator cunning

MISSION

97

Fool your friends into thinking you can see into the future.

1 Grab a calculator and a piece of paper.

2 Write "13" on the paper, fold it up and give it to a friend, but tell him not to look at it yet.

3 Ask your friend to give you a three-digit number.

4 Letting your friend watch, type the number into your calculator twice – for example, 234234.

5 Tell your friend that you know just by looking that this number is divisible by 77.

6 Divide by 77, then divide by your friend's original three-digit number and hit the equal sign.

7 Tell your friend to check the piece of paper.

8 The answer on the calculator will be 13 and will match the number on the paper!

Don't perform this mission twice on the same person or your ruse may be rumbled!

MISSION ACCEPTED | MONTH | DAY | YEAR

98 Hazard map

A hazard map plots a route you frequently take – for example, to a friend's house – and all the potential dangers and obstacles along the way. Design your own hazard map here.

Be sure to include:
1. Your start and finish points.
2. Any secret shortcuts.
3. The spookiest house on the street.
4. Where there is always something nasty on the pavement.
5. Your favorite bench or a weird-looking tree.
6. The house with a scary dog.
7. The best bush to hide behind.

MISSION ACCEPTED

MONTH	DAY	YEAR

Hoop glider

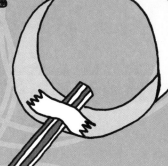

MISSION
99

This amazing glider is made in minutes!

1 Find some stiff paper or card and cut it into two strips measuring 0.8 in (2 cm) by 6 in (15 cm).

2 Curl the strips into two hoops, one bigger than the other, and tape them together.

3 Tape the hoops to the straw, making sure the straw sits inside the hoops.

4 You have your glider! Hold the straw in the middle and throw it into the air like a javelin or dart.

TOP TIPS

• Add designs to the strips of paper and experiment with different sized hoops and straw lengths.

• Try hiding a rolled-up secret message in the straw.

MISSION

ULTIMATE mission! 100

Imagine the coolest mission ever – log it here:

Would you travel forward or backward in time?

Where would you go?

What type of transportation would take you there?

What would you take with you?

Who would go with you?

What would you do?

MISSION ACCEPTED

MONTH	DAY	YEAR

ANSWERS

Check your answers here.

Mission 4

1 5 2 6 3 7 4 8 5

Mission 22

There are 19 squares, including:

12 (1 x 1) squares

5 (2 x 2) squares

2 (3 x 3) squares

Mission 31

There is just one rope.

Mission 34

Mission 41

Yellow – the colors are in alphabetical order.

Mission 43

A Z C X E V G T I R

Mission 45

TEN

Mission 49

The agents will enter the mansion at nine-thirty.

Mission 59

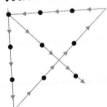

Mission 64

The dog-eared weevil and flat-tailed mountain duck are not real animals.

Mission 73

Mission 76
The first letter in each word spells the agent's name, Adam Brown.

Mission 79
The snowman melted.

Mission 80

Mission 84
The barbers cut each other's hair, so you should go to Pete to get a nice, neat cut.

Mission 85
Shoes.

Mission 94
There are 48 beans.